Arthur and the No-Brainer

A Marc Brown ARTHUR Chapter Book

Arthur and the No-Brainer

Text by Stephen Krensky

Based on a teleplay by Dietrich Smith

Little, Brown and Company

Boston   New York   London

First Edition

The characters and events portrayed in this book are fictitious. Any
similarity to real persons, living or dead, is coincidental and not intended
by the author.

Text has been reviewed and assigned a reading level by Laurel S. Ernst,
M.A., Teachers College, Columbia University, New York, New York;
reading specialist, Chappaqua, New York.

ISBN 0-316-12332-3 (hc) / ISBN 0-316-12132-0 (pb)

Library of Congress Control Number 2002102898

10   9   8   7   6   5   4   3   2   1

WOR (hc)
COM-MO (pb)

Printed in the United States of America

Chapter 1

Mr. Ratburn stood in front of his third-grade class, smiling.

"Relax, everyone. There's no reason to be nervous."

His words sounded calm and reasonable, but they made no difference. The look of fear on everyone's face remained unchanged. All eyes were focused on the bunch of straws Mr. Ratburn was holding in his hand. The ends sticking out of the top were all the same length, but on the bottom — the hidden end — one straw was short.

"Who will pick the short straw?" Mr.

Ratburn asked. "Whom will Lady Luck smile on today? Will it be you, Francine?" He held out his hand toward her.

Francine gulped. She squeezed her eyes shut and picked out a straw. It was a long one.

"Ahhhh," she sighed, smiling with relief.

Mr. Ratburn shook his head. "May I take this opportunity to remind everyone that this is not some kind of punishment?"

Arthur and Buster shared a look. That was easy for Mr. Ratburn to say. After all, he wasn't the one doing the picking.

Binky was next. "Gee, this is a big moment," he said. "Maybe I should be better prepared."

"Choose, please, Binky," said Mr. Ratburn.

"Being prepared is very important," Binky went on. "As you're always telling us. And you know how I take in every word —"

"Binky!"

"Okay, okay. Sheeesh. Eeny, meeney, miney . . . mo!"

He picked — and his was a long straw, too.

Sue Ellen and Muffy followed, and their straws were long as well.

"Please keep the groaning to a minimum," Mr. Ratburn told the remaining class members. "It really doesn't have to be this way. We can stop right now if anyone wants to volunteer for the task at hand."

Nobody raised a hand. And so Mr. Ratburn continued. As he walked around the room, straw after straw was picked.

They were all long ones.

Finally, Mr. Ratburn came to Arthur and Buster.

"I guess it's come down to you two," he said. "Two straws. Two students. One long and one short. Are you ready?"

Arthur didn't look ready. He looked like he would rather be at the dentist having a tooth pulled. Buster looked even worse. Two teeth at least. Or maybe three.

"Don't be shy, boys. Make your move."

Both Arthur and Buster were sweating. They were thinking the same thing — why couldn't somebody else have picked the short straw earlier? Then they could have been sympathetic, patting whomever it was on the back and making supportive remarks. Instead, that was what everyone else was going to do to one of them. Arthur reached out slowly and touched the top of the two straws. Back and forth went his fingers, unable to make a decision.

Then Buster cracked. He made a sudden

lunge and grabbed a straw — the short one.

"Aieeeeeeee!"

"Congratulations, Buster!" said Mr. Ratburn, beaming. "You win."

"Win?" Buster gasped. "You call competing against the Brain in a math contest winning? Well, I don't."

And then he fell back in his chair like a wet noodle.

Chapter 2

• • • • • • • • • • •

Mr. Ratburn stood on the left side of the auditorium stage staring out at the students. To his right, Buster and the Brain stood at podiums, waiting for the questions to begin.

The Brain flexed his fingers and then covered his mouth as a yawn tried to escape.

Meanwhile, Buster was frantically flipping through joke books. "If I can make the crowd laugh," he muttered, "maybe it won't matter that I don't know anything."

"It's just a contest, Buster," said the

Brain. "If you get a question wrong, it's not the end of the world."

"How would you know? You never get questions wrong. Maybe it's more like the end of the world than you think."

"All right, contestants," said Mr. Ratburn, "please remove all reference materials so we can begin."

Francine stepped forward and took away Buster's joke books.

"Are we ready for the first question?" Mr. Ratburn went on.

"Go easy, Brain . . . please," Buster whispered.

Mr. Ratburn cleared his throat. "Define *hypotenuse.*"

Buster pressed his buzzer at once. *BZZZZZZZ!*

"Yes, Buster?" said Mr. Ratburn.

"I . . . no . . . I . . . did I do that?"

Mr. Ratburn folded his arms. "Yes, you did. And you have five seconds to answer."

Buster smiled awkwardly. Then he started waving madly. "Hi, Potenuse!" he shouted.

The audience laughed.

Mr. Ratburn allowed himself a small smile. "Very amusing, Buster, but we're not performing at Jack's Joke Shop. All right, Brain, would you like to try?"

The Brain hesitated for a moment. "Um, can I pass?" he asked.

Mr. Ratburn looked surprised. "If you'd like."

Hey, what are you doing? said a voice inside the Brain's head. *I know, I know, you're worried about Buster. Well, don't be. He'll be fine. Meanwhile, millions of people will think you don't know what a hypotenuse is.*

The Brain sighed. "Excuse me, Mr. Ratburn. I've changed my mind. A hypotenuse is the side of a trapezoid."

"I'm sorry," said Mr. Ratburn. "That's incorrect."

The audience gasped.

The Brain was shocked.

Wrong? said the voice in the Brain's head. *We're never wrong.*

While the Brain was busy thinking, he missed Mr. Ratburn's next question. Buster hit his buzzer.

"Yes, Buster?" said Mr. Ratburn.

Buster looked excited. "I know this one. An octagon has eight arms, er . . . I mean, sides."

"Correct."

Buster smiled. "Good thing I watched *Attack of the Octopus People* last night!"

"Next," said Mr. Ratburn. "Jack and Jill went to the ice-cream parlor. There was a special that day that added one free scoop for every two scoops you bought. If Jack bought the Leaning Tower four-scoop supreme, how many —"

BZZZZZZ!

"Six!" said Buster, licking his lips.

"Especially if it's the double chocolate almond ripple."

"Correct!" said Mr. Ratburn.

"But you didn't finish the question," said the Brain.

"The rules don't say anything about that," Mr. Ratburn explained. "If Buster wants to take a chance, that's his option. You, of course, are free to do the same."

"But I like to hear the whole question in case there are any subtleties."

Mr. Ratburn nodded. "Then you're taking a chance of a different kind."

The Brain looked as if he didn't like the sound of that.

Chapter 3

"I BEAT THE BRAIN!" Buster shouted at the top of his lungs as he pushed open the school doors at the end of the day.

The other kids followed him out to the playground.

"Way to go, Buster!"

"You were unbelievable!"

"Eating all that ice cream was bound to pay off someday!"

As Buster went off with the admiring crowd, Arthur, Muffy, and the Brain brought up the rear. Arthur was happy for Buster, of course, but he was concerned about the Brain.

The Brain didn't look concerned. He didn't look anything, really.

"I don't understand, Brain," said Arthur. "You've never had any trouble with those kinds of questions before. But once Buster answered that octagon thing, you weren't the same. Buster got hotter and hotter and you just, well, crumbled. You barely got any questions right at all."

"Crumbled . . . ," the Brain repeated. "Little tiny pieces . . . microscopic . . . smaller than grains of sand . . . crumbled to the atomic level . . . subatomic, even. Very small."

"Yes, yes," said Arthur. "Well, it wasn't that bad."

"Crumble, mumble, stumble," muttered the Brain. "They all go together. Have you ever noticed that?"

Arthur rolled his eyes. "Can't say that I have. But that doesn't explain what happened."

The Brain continued to stare straight ahead. "What happened? . . . Too many things have happened since the dawn of time to mention them all in one . . ."

"Hell-oooo," said Muffy. "Earth to Brain. Come in, Brain. Red alert."

"Why only red?" the Brain said absently. "So many colors to choose from."

He wandered away toward the bikes.

"Houston, we have a problem," said Muffy. "Do you think it's safe to leave him alone?"

Arthur frowned. "I'd feel better if he were blinking more."

Francine jogged over. She had listened to Buster get more than enough compliments.

"Don't worry," she said to Arthur and Muffy. "I can handle this."

Francine approached the Brain near the bikes. "Hey, Brain. Tough break today. But, you know, the world is filled with tough breaks. I mean, if it weren't, we wouldn't know they were tough. All the breaks would just be soft or easy or whatever it is that breaks are when they're not tough. Right?"

The Brain didn't answer.

Francine took a deep breath. "Anyway, the point is, you can't let tough breaks get to you. You have to fix them or forget them or do something so that they don't get to you."

The Brain still said nothing.

Francine raised her hand and knocked gently on the side of the Brain's head. "Anybody home in there?"

"Stop it, Francine," said Arthur. "I know you're trying to help, but —"

The Brain started to walk away. "See you guys later. I have to get home. I think I hear my mother calling me."

Francine, Arthur, and Muffy watched

him go. Arthur hadn't heard anything. Neither had the others.

"Gee," said Francine, "this is worse than I thought."

Chapter 4

• • • • • • • • • • •

That night at dinner, the Brain didn't have much of an appetite. He had shaped his mashed potatoes into a pyramid.

"Historically noteworthy," his father observed. "But I believe the goal here is to eat them."

The Brain nodded slowly and scooped up a forkful.

"You don't seem very hungry," said his mother. "Are you feeling okay? Did you have a good day at school?"

"Chimerical," said the Brain.

His mother exchanged a glance with his father. Then she got up and retrieved a fat dictionary from the counter. They flipped quickly through the pages.

The Brain's father coughed. "And what made your day like 'a fire-breathing monster with a lion's head and a goat's body'?"

"I think he must mean definition number two," said the Brain's mother.

"Ah. Absurd or impossible. So, what made your day like that?"

The Brain sighed. "Lots of things. What would you think of me if I ever got anything wrong?"

His mother smiled. "Well, honey, everybody gets things wrong sometimes."

"I suppose that's true," said the Brain, considering it. "The occasional exception only proves the rule."

"Exactly."

"So if I got something wrong, you wouldn't be disappointed?"

His mother smiled. "The sun would still

come up in the morning," she reminded him.

The Brain nodded. "I guess I was just tired."

"You're sure you're not coming down with anything?" his mother asked. She placed a hand on his forehead.

"No, no. I don't have that excuse." The Brain stood up. "Maybe I should go do some homework."

"Good idea," said his mother. "That always perks you up."

Up in his bedroom, the Brain settled down to read. Some people liked to read stretched out on their beds, but not the Brain. He sat at his desk, his notepad ready — in case he wanted to write anything down.

But he had trouble concentrating. The day's events kept playing themselves over and over in his mind. He was very tired, and his head soon slumped forward.

In a hospital room, a doctor was reading a chart on an EEG machine. Mr. Ratburn was assisting. Next to the machine, the Brain was lying in bed.

"I.Q. at one twenty and still falling. . . . One eighteen . . . one fifteen."

"What does that mean?" asked the Brain's father, who was standing nearby with the Brain's mother.

"I'm afraid his intelligence is in free fall," the doctor explained. "It's not life-threatening. He's in no immediate danger, except, of course, the danger of becoming average."

The Brain's parents gasped.

"Average?" his father repeated. "You mean, he will become of ordinary intelligence?"

The doctor nodded. "I'm afraid so. We can work medical miracles today in many areas, but the brain remains the last frontier." He turned to Mr. Ratburn. "Want to call it?"

Mr. Ratburn looked at his watch. "Four fifty-three P.M. *The patient was declared average."*

The Brain's head jerked up as he suddenly awoke. "Average," he muttered, staring sadly out the window. "That's what I am." *Clearly,* he thought, *it is the beginning of the end.*

Chapter 5

• • • • • • • • • • • •

Buster was sitting on the floor at home, eating a huge banana split and watching the sci-fi classic *Heads of Lettuce Will Roll.* His mother had made him a special dessert to celebrate the big news.

"I'm very proud of you, Buster," she said. "Being chosen to represent your class in the school mathathon is quite an accomplishment. Maybe my newspaper should cover the event. It's a good human-interest story."

Buster smiled. He had been in the newspaper before, but never for using his head.

"How did the Brain react?" asked Mrs. Baxter. "If I remember correctly, he's always been the one to represent your class."

Buster shrugged. "Actually, the Brain was out today. Arthur thought that was a little weird, because the Brain is never sick. But Francine said that everyone gets sick sometimes."

He took a spoonful of ice cream.

"Well," said Mrs. Baxter, "I'm sure it's nothing serious. I'm sure you'll see him soon enough."

Buster nodded and continued eating. He was just scraping the bottom of his bowl when the doorbell rang.

"I'll get it!" Buster shouted.

He ran to the door and opened it.

It was the Brain.

"Wow!" said Buster. "My mother really knows what she's talking about."

"I'm glad to hear it," said the Brain. "But

that's not why I'm here. I've brought you some things."

"I thought you were sick," said Buster.

"I've made a miraculous recovery."

Buster nodded. "I made one of those once. But my mom said it was a little odd, coming just after a big test at school."

"Mine wasn't like that," the Brain insisted.

"No, no, of course not. Tests don't bother you." Buster frowned. "What's that you're pulling?"

The Brain stepped aside to give Buster a better look. It was a big cart piled high with books, beakers, a telescope, and a microscope.

"Arthur called," the Brain explained. "He told me Mr. Ratburn chose you for the mathathon. Congratulations."

"Thanks." Buster took a closer look at the cart. "Hey, I recognize this stuff. You've used it to figure out some pretty tricky problems."

"True," the Brain admitted. "But my problem-solving days are over. So I really don't need this stuff anymore. That's why I'm giving it all to you."

"Me?" Buster squeaked. "Why me?"

"You're a brain now," said the Brain. "And a brain needs these things."

"I do?" Buster frowned. "I had no idea." He picked up one of the books and opened it. "Gee, this print is pretty small. And no pictures, either."

The Brain ran a hand gently over the telescope. "You'll take good care of everything, right?"

"Oh, sure." Buster patted the microscope. "No worries, there. You can depend on me. And why? Because I'm dependable."

"Okay," said the Brain. "Well, I've got to be going."

"Are you sure you don't want to come in? I'm watching *Heads of Lettuce Will Roll,* and it's just getting to the good part, where all of the evil lettuce heads get turned into this enormous salad."

"No, no, I've got to get back."

And with one last look at his cart, the Brain turned and walked away.

Chapter 6

• • • • • • • • • • •

Arthur and Francine were talking on the playground.

"It definitely feels weird," said Arthur.

Francine nodded. "Not just weird. Superweird."

"Weirder than weird," Arthur went on. "I mean, the Brain has been part of the school mathathon for as long as I can remember. He always looked forward to it. He'd get that little gleam in his eye. And he'd start mumbling different numbers in the hall."

"Yeah," said Francine. "And we used to

race him against the school calculators for practice."

"It's hard to believe those days are gone," said Arthur. "Things sure move fast sometimes. Now everything's changed. Now, Buster is —"

"What about me?" asked Buster, coming up behind them.

"Oh, hi, Buster. We were, um, just saying how different it is having you in the mathathon. Not bad, just different."

"I know." Buster smiled. "It's different for me, too. Who would ever have thought I'd be replacing the Brain?"

"Not me," said Francine. "Hey, what's all that stuff?" She pointed to the cart he was pulling.

"You know," said Arthur, "the Brain has a telescope just like that."

"Actually, he doesn't," said Buster. "Not anymore."

"Really? It looks the same."

"That's because it is the same," Buster explained. "Alan gave it to me, along with everything else."

"No way," said Francine. She took a closer look. "Gee, these are his favorite books . . . and his lab equipment. . . ."

"I know," said Buster. "Alan said that he wouldn't need any of this stuff anymore, and that he should pass it along to someone who could use it."

Francine frowned. "So why did he give it to you?"

"Because he thought I would want it."

Francine started laughing. "No, really."

"I'm serious," said Buster. "That's what he said. So I thought I'd carry this stuff around — just in case."

"Come on, Buster," said Francine. "You may have beaten the Brain once, but think about your grades, and your —"

"Grades don't mean everything," Buster insisted. "Alan said that Albert Ein-

stein didn't always get great grades when he was in school, either."

"Einstein?"

Buster shrugged. "Some genius who figured out stuff about light and gravity. Alan explained it to me."

Arthur frowned. "Why do you keep calling him 'Alan'?"

"He said not to call him the Brain anymore. He said that there wasn't any point in it. That it was ancient history. He said to use his regular name."

"But only his mother calls him Alan," said Francine. "We couldn't do that unless . . ."

She paled.

"Unless he really wasn't a brain anymore," Arthur finished for her.

They looked at each other in shock.

Chapter 7

●●●●●●●●●●●●

"Welcome to the show," the Brain said to an audience of action figures and stuffed animals that he had arranged on his bed.

"Thank you all for coming. As you know, comics often test out their material by popping into comedy clubs unannounced. It is in that spirit that I appear before you today. And aside from the fact that you are a collection of inanimate objects, and I am performing in my bedroom, there's hardly any difference."

He took a deep breath.

"So what's the idea with cafeteria food? Half the time we receive mystery meat, but the only mystery is where that green color really comes from. Excuuuse me, but if I want slop, I can read Ogleberg's treatise on binomial coefficients. And how about those substitute teachers —"

Knock, knock.

"Come in," said the Brain.

Arthur, Francine, and Buster opened the door.

"Uh, hi, Brain," said Arthur. "Your mother let us in. Can we talk?"

"Sure. But it's Alan now, Arthur. That Brain stuff is a thing of the past."

"Yeah, yeah," said Francine. "We heard." She looked at the figures lined up on the bed. "So what are you doing?"

The Brain turned slightly red. "Well, now that things have changed, I need to be practical. Can't mope about the past. That's why I'm training for a new career."

"As what?" asked Arthur.

"A comedian."

Francine laughed. "Now that's funny."

The Brain shook his head. "I'm perfectly serious. If academic pursuits are closed to me, I must investigate other possibilities."

"Isn't comedy kind of a stretch, though?" asked Francine.

"No, no. Comedy seems like a natural choice, because it doesn't require great intelligence."

"Hey!" cried Buster. "Jokes are not dumb. Well, except for dumb jokes, but that's different because they're supposed to be that way."

"I don't just tell jokes," the Brain said. "There's physical humor, too. Watch this." He took a giant inflatable mallet out of a trunk. Then he walloped the top of the table.

"Do you know what I just did?" the Brain asked. "I just smashed an atom."

Everyone stared blankly at him.

"Get it? Smashed an atom?"

"We get it," said Arthur. "It's just not funny. Anyway, one contest is not a reason to give up."

The Brain sighed. "Everything comes to an end eventually. I can see the handwriting on the wall — and in half a dozen languages. Besides, you don't need me as your brain. You have Buster."

"It's not the same," said Arthur.

"This is c-crazy!" Francine sputtered.

The Brain shrugged. "I'm just being practical — and willing to face the facts." He took a baby doll and a milk pitcher out of the trunk next. "Now, I know there's a good one here about not crying over spilled milk. I just have to work out the kinks. So if you'll excuse me, I have to rehearse."

He ushered them out in silence, because nobody knew what else to say.

Chapter 8

The next day Arthur, Francine, and Buster followed the Brain after school.

"We're not spying on him," Francine explained. "We're just making sure he's all right. The Brain hasn't been himself lately."

The others nodded.

It was not hard to follow the Brain, because he made no attempt to hide or hurry. He simply headed directly for Jack's Joke Shop.

His followers watched from across the street.

"One of my favorite places," said Buster.

"Maybe I should go inside and check on him."

"No, no," said Arthur. "We don't want him to think we're worried about him. And if he bumps into us, that's just what he'll think."

"Okay, okay," said Buster. "I'll stay here."

"He's really taking this whole comic thing seriously," said Francine.

"Only the Brain would take being funny seriously," Buster pointed out.

"We've got to get him back to normal," said Arthur. "His confidence has been shaken. We need to build it up again."

"As soon as possible," said Francine. "A class without a brain is like —"

"Hey!" said Buster. "Wait a minute. What about me? What makes you think I can't be a brain, too?"

Francine grabbed a book from the

Brain's cart and flipped through some pages. "If x equals pi times y cubed, and y equals the square root of seventy-eight, how would you solve for x?"

"Easy," said Buster.

"Really?" Arthur and Francine said together.

Buster nodded. "I'd just ask the Brain."

"And are you going to do that during the mathathon?" Francine asked.

"No. Then I'll have to answer the questions . . . for myself." Buster turned pale. "I'm doomed!"

"Don't panic," said Francine. "I'm sure we can figure something out."

"Maybe we could trick the Brain into solving some problems," said Arthur. "Then he might snap out of it."

"You really think that will work?" Francine asked.

"I don't know," Arthur admitted. "But it's worth a try."

*   *   *

That night the Brain laid out his new props on his bed. There was a curly red wig, a pair of two-foot-long shoes, and a flower that squirted water.

"Tools of the trade," he said to himself. "They'll work nicely into my new routine."

Rinnnggggggg.

He answered the phone.

"Hello?"

"Yes," said a deep voice on the other end of the line. "Is the brain of the house in?"

"Um, you may have the wrong —"

"Nonsense, sir. You sound like the right person to me. This is a most fortunate day for you. We here at the Nevermind Institute are prepared to offer you a free trip to Einstein's birthplace. All you have to do is answer a few questions. Now listen carefully. Determine the value of x if a —"

45

"Arthur, this is not going to work," said the Brain.

Then he hung up.

Chapter 9

• • • • • • • • • • • •

Arthur, Francine, and Buster were sitting in the back of the ice-cream parlor. Some of the chairs and tables had been pulled away to make room for a performance.

The performer was the Brain. He was going to give his first show before a live audience, and he had asked his friends to be there.

"Do you think this will be any good?" Francine whispered.

Arthur didn't look hopeful. "Not if he's going to use that inflatable mallet again."

"Really?" said Buster. "I kind of liked that."

"I wish he would just be the old Brain again," said Arthur. "We tried everything . . . and none of it worked."

"So it's over?" said Francine. "We're giving up?"

"Not yet," said Arthur. "We've still got the secret weapon."

"The secret weapon?" said Buster. "Nobody told me about a secret weapon."

"Because then it wouldn't be a secret," Arthur explained.

Buster wanted to know more, but the Brain was calling for their attention. He was wearing his new wig, baggy pants, and floppy shoes. But somehow he really didn't look very comfortable.

"Thank you all for coming," he said. "I know you're out there. I can hear your pulmonary systems in action."

"What?" whispered Buster.

"He means we're breathing," Arthur explained.

"So, um, let's begin. . . . I hope you'll cut me some slack because I'm self-taut."

Silence.

"See," the Brain explained, "*taut* means tight, but it also sounds like *taught,* as in self-taught. Oh, never mind."

Suddenly, a young girl burst into the ice-cream parlor. She had long pigtails and giant freckles.

"Is there a mathematician in the house?" she cried.

Everyone in the audience looked at the Brain.

The Brain turned to her. "I used to be," he admitted.

"You look very mathy, that's for sure. You've got to help — and quick!"

"Why? What's happened?"

"Well, this train left Denver at noon going seventy-five miles an hour. But then this other train left Miami."

The Brain narrowed his eyes and looked harder at her.

"Nice try, D.W., but I don't think that —"

At that moment, a book fell out of his baggy pants onto the floor.

"Hey!" said Buster. "I recognize that. It's a math book. You haven't given up being the Brain. You're sneaking math books."

"No, I . . . I . . . It's just a prop!" the Brain said.

Arthur and Francine folded their arms.

"Are you saying math is a joke?" asked Arthur.

The Brain gasped. "I would never say that."

"Then what are you saying?" asked Francine, with a small smile.

The Brain sighed and pulled off his wig. "Okay, okay," he said. "You're right. I don't really want to do this. I want to do the mathathon — no matter how scary it is."

"Hooray!" said Arthur. "Thank goodness you've come to your senses."

"But I'm sure it's too late," said the Brain.

"No, don't worry," said Buster. "You can have my place."

"Oh, I couldn't do that," said the Brain.

"Please," said Buster. "Don't make me beg. It's not a pretty sight."

"All right," said the Brain. "If that's the way you feel about it, let's see what we can do."

Chapter 10

• • • • • • • • • • • •

"I believe we are ready to begin," Mr. Haney, the school principal, said to start the Lakewood Elementary Mathathon. Near him on the auditorium stage, the first contestants were ready to go.

One of them was the Brain. As he stood ready, the inside of his head was trying to stay calm. "Don't be nervous. . . . Knock 'em dead, kid. . . . Hit one out of the park. . . ."

His friends were sitting in the front row. They all looked nervous, too, except for Buster, who looked relieved that Mr. Ratburn had let the Brain take his place.

"Define pi," said Mr. Haney.

The Brain took a deep breath. "Um . . . the ratio of the circumference of a circle to its diameter."

"Correct."

Mr. Ratburn's class cheered, and the Brain allowed himself a small smile.

"Next question," said Mr. Haney, and the Brain let out a sigh. With the first question behind him, he felt like his old self again. He didn't know if he would win or lose, but he was confident of one thing. Like the chicken that crossed the road, he would make it safely to the other side.